Praise for Storyshares

"One of the brightest innovators and game-changers in the education industry."
— Forbes

"Your success in applying research-validated practices to promote literacy serves as a valuable model for other organizations seeking to create evidence-based literacy programs."
— Library of Congress

"We need powerful social and educational innovation, and Storyshares is breaking new ground. The organization addresses critical problems facing our students and teachers. I am excited about the strategies it brings to the collective work of making sure every student has an equal chance in life."
— Teach For America

"It's the perfect idea. There's really nothing like this. I mean, wow, this will be a wonderful experience for young people."
— Andrea Davis Pinkney, Executive Director, Scholastic

"Reading for meaning opens opportunities for a lifetime of learning. Providing emerging readers with engaging texts that are designed to offer both challenges and support for each individual will improve their lives for years to come. Storyshares is a wonderful start."
— David Rose, Co-founder of CAST & UDL

The Detail

Storyshares presents

Published by Storyshares, LLC

Storyshares
Storyshares, LLC
24 N. Bryn Mawr Avenue #340
Bryn Mawr, Pennsylvania 19010-3304
www.storyshares.org

Inspiring reading with a new kind of book.

Interest Level: High School
Grade Level Equivalent: 3.9

ISBN 9798885977555
Book design by Saskia Globig

THE DETAIL

David Agard

Storyshares

CONTENTS

CHAPTER ONE

When we grow old, we spend time reflecting on our lives. I don't know which is more complicated, regretting our mistakes and bad choices or regretting what we did not do.

A regret that haunts me is *Why didn't I hug and comfort Arnold?*

I wondered if I could find him and give him a past-due hug.

CHAPTER TWO

1954

We lived thirty-five miles away from Chicago in a rural community. My dad asked me to go there with him to pick up a part for his tractor. It was my first trip to Chicago that I remembered.

When we entered the city, I saw a strange-looking woman.

"Look, Dad, there's a chocolate lady," I said.

Dad laughed a little. "No, son, she has dark skin," he said. "They were brought here from Africa. We are vanilla-skinned people, and we came here from Europe."

Over the years, our community grew. Dad had to sell our eighty-acre farm because it couldn't support a baby-boom family of six. He broke even on the sale and got a job as a welder in a factory. Three-bedroom ranch houses popped up on the old farm faster than corn because people were moving out of Chicago. Only white people moved here.

Television brought the world, including Black people, into our suburban homes. By the middle 1960s, there was Gayle Sayers of the Bears, my favorite sports hero. My dad was a boxing fan. He liked Cassius Clay until he changed his name to Muhammad Ali and refused the draft.

The evening news showed Black people holding signs and marching in the South. The news also showed Martin Luther King delivering speeches about freedom.

CHAPTER THREE

January, 1968

Since I wasn't college material, I got drafted.

The night before I left for the Army, the family had a special dinner for me. There were three courses: the main course, dessert, and advice served last.

Mom said, "Make friends with the nearest boy to you. They'll be lonely for home, too."

Dad was a World War Two veteran. He said, "Don't volunteer for any detail, stay small, and for God's sake, don't get killed. Your brother is there now, and we worry and pray for him daily."

After basic training, they sent me to Fort Jack-

son, South Carolina for advanced infantry training.
In basic training, one in ten were Black guys. But in
infantry training, there were two in ten.

On our first day there, we settled in our barracks.
A Black guy found the bunk above me. We looked
at each other's nametags, sewn on our shirts. I was
Olsen, and he was Arnold.

I didn't remember his first name. His last name
sounded like a first name, anyway. We did the
"Where are you from?" introduction routine. He was
from Ohio and I was from Illinois. Remembering my
mom's advice, Arnold and I became friends.

We both had older brothers who were in Vietnam.
We both smoked, and shared our cigarettes when
the other was out. A sign of an actual buddy.

He showed me a picture of his girlfriend. I
showed him a picture of my girlfriend. Both photos
were wallet-sized and placed in plastic holders.

On weekend leave, we took a bus to Myrtle
Beach. We got drunk and got tattoos of a tiger's
head on our shoulders. I got a sunburn. Arnold
did not.

Each day after training, we marched back to the
company area, where we stood in formation. The
First Sergeant shouted out information about this,
that, and the other thing.

Yeah, yeah, yeah, I thought.

After that was mail call. Arnold got a letter from his girl back home. I got a letter from my girl. At chow, Arnold and I sat together.

In the evening, we hung out together. We studied our manuals, took care of our equipment, shined our boots, and talked about home. Arnold told me stories. I told him stories.

We were friends.

CHAPTER FOUR

On April 4th, word spread that Martin Luther King, Jr. had been assassinated. The Army put the entire fort on lockdown and we were confined to our barracks.

The Black guys huddled together. Some cried and some ranted. Right before lights out, Arnold returned to his bunk. He looked at me with watery eyes.

"Olsen, some white guy shot him," he said. "We'll never be free."

I didn't understand his pain, but he was my friend. I wanted to comfort him. I didn't know how, though.

After a couple of days, we returned to doing our daily routines together. We were friends.

One afternoon, the Captain came to the day-ending formation. We were especially quick at snapping to attention because he rarely graced us with his presence.

After the First Sergeant shouted his daily information, the Captain stepped forward. He said, "Private Arnold, fall out and report to me."

Yikes, Arnold, I thought. *What the heck did you do?*

Arnold left the formation and reported to the Captain. After a brief conversation with Arnold, the Captain asked, "Who wants to go with Arnold on a special detail?"

I heard my dad's voice. *Don't volunteer for anything.* But without hesitation I shouted, "I will, sir."

Arnold was my friend.

CHAPTER FIVE

I reported to the Captain. He gave Arnold and me the at-ease command.

The Captain looked at my nametag. He said to me, "Olsen, I want you to escort Arnold to the Red Cross. Listen up. You stay with Arnold until the detail is done. They'll tell you more when you get there. Do you understand?"

I answered sharply, "Yes, sir." But I did wonder, *What do you mean, "until the detail is done?"*

I didn't ask questions, and the Captain didn't give me a chance. He quickly dismissed us. We snapped to attention and gave a salute. He returned the salute and walked away.

"What do you think this is about?" Arnold asked me.

"I don't know," I said. I was still processing the Captain's orders.

We walked a little while in silence. Then Arnold asked again,"Why do you think I have to go to the Red Cross?"

I had been thinking about it. I could not think of a reason, but I sensed it was not good. They were not giving us free beer, throwing us a belated birthday party, or flying our girlfriends down for a weekend rendezvous.

He kept asking, "Why do you think I have to go to the Red Cross?"

I kept answering, "I don't know."

He asked and I answered at least ten times. In between was silence.

CHAPTER SIX

We finally arrived at the Red Cross. They seemed to be waiting for us.

A Red Cross worker quickly took us into a room and told us to have a seat. Soon after, an Army Chaplain came in through another door. We started to get up to salute, but he motioned for us to stay seated.

For the first time in my life, I saw the shiny, razor-sharp sword of grief and pain in the Chaplain's expression. They say sharp blades cut fast, with less pain and more mercy.

With no warning, the Chaplain drove the sword into Arnold's heart. "Private Arnold," he said. "We regret to inform you that your brother was killed in action yesterday."

It took Arnold about ten seconds to feel the sword. Then he burst into tears, arching his shoulders up and down with each sob.

Big boys don't cry, I thought.

The Chaplain went around the table and put his hand on Arnold's shoulder. "I'm sorry, son," he said.

I did not know what to do, because I had never witnessed such a thing.

The following ten minutes seemed like an eternity. Arnold finally paused to come up for air. The Chaplain explained that the Red Cross would fly him home for the funeral so he could be with his family. He said Arnold would be recycled with another company to finish his training when he returned to duty. He then gave Arnold some generic words of condolence.

Sadly, I didn't know how to offer anything better.

The Chaplain looked at me, then my nametag.

"Private Olsen, you help Arnold gather his gear and check him out of the company," he said.

They took us back to the barracks in a car. Arnold's sobbing was interrupted by short periods of silence.

I helped him gather his gear and carry it to the waiting car. He got in the car and hung his head. I said goodbye as I closed the door, but I don't think he heard me.

The car pulled away. Arnold was gone, and so was my innocence.

CHAPTER SEVEN

After searching a pay-for-use database, I finally found Arnold. His first name was Thomas. Two first names.

I drove to Westlake, Ohio, a suburb of Cleveland, Ohio. I parked in front of his well-kept ranch-style house.

Maybe he wouldn't remember me. Maybe he didn't think I cared.

Suddenly, the garage door opened. An old Black man pushed a lawnmower onto the driveway. I got out of the car and walked up the driveway. Arnold watched me cautiously, wondering what the old white guy wanted.

When I got close to Arnold, I rolled up my sleeve to show the tattoo of a tiger's head on my shoulder.

"Hi, Arnold," I said. "Remember me? Olsen."

Arnold stood in silence, looking at me and thinking back in time.

Finally, he said, "Yeah, I remember you from Fort Jackson." Our eyes welled up with tears.

Speechless, I walked to Arnold. We embraced, and I gave him the hug I owed him for over fifty years.

I caught my breath. "I'm so sorry you lost your brother," I said.

After several pats on the back, we let go.

Arnold looked at me with watery eyes. "I always wanted to thank you for volunteering to come with me that day I found out my brother was killed," he said.

We hugged each other again.

We are friends.

About the Author

David Agard is a contributing author to the Storyshares library.

About the Publisher

Storyshares is a publisher focused on supporting the millions of teens and adults who struggle with reading by creating a new shelf in the library specifically for them. The ever-growing collection features content that is compelling and culturally relevant for teens and adults, yet still readable at a range of lower reading levels.

Storyshares generates content by engaging deeply with writers, bringing together a community to create this new kind of book. With more intriguing and approachable stories to choose from, the teens and adults who have fallen behind are improving their skills and beginning to discover the joy of reading.

For more information, visit storyshares.org.

Easy to Read. Hard to Put Down.

www.ingramcontent.com/pod-product-compliance
Lightning Source LLC
Chambersburg PA
CBHW071231170626
46809CB00005BA/2032